# WHO HAS SEEN
## THE BEAST?

*Anne Schraff*

SADDLEBACK
PAGETURNERS
•ADVENTURE•

# PAGETURNERS

**ADVENTURE**

**MYSTERY**

Development and Production: Laurel Associates, Inc.
Cover Illustrator: Black Eagle Productions

SADDLEBACK
PUBLISHING · INC.
Three Watson
Irvine, CA 92618-2767

E-Mail: info@sdlback.com
Website: www.sdlback.com

ISBN 1-56254-186-2

Printed in the United States of America
05 04 03 02 01 00    9 8 7 6 5 4 3 2 1

# CONTENTS

# Chapter 1

Lettie Marin and her parents had been planning a mountain camping trip at Owl Lake for three years. It was to be a kind of family celebration. Lettie had just finished high school, and her brother, Jacob, had completed two years of community college. Now it was late June. The family had rented a camper, and at last they were headed out for the high country.

"We probably won't find a decent camping site very close to the lake," Dad said as the camper climbed the winding mountain road. "*Everybody* wants the lakeside spots this time of year. We should have called a lot earlier for reservations."

But they were in luck. Just as the

Marin family neared the lake, another family was vacating a choice site. It was an isolated, beautiful spot with a clear view of the lake through the pine trees. "Man, this is great!" Jacob yelled.

"You guys really pulling out?" Dad called from the cab of the camper. He couldn't believe it.

"Yeah, we sure are," a middle-aged man said. He was pulling down a big tent while his sons were throwing their gear into a van. They all seemed to be in a mad rush. "You're welcome to this place!"

Mom laughed. "Looks like they just remembered it was the last day of their vacation!"

"Wow," Lettie sighed happily as she looked around, "you can even see the snowcapped mountains in the distance. This is like paradise!" She was so entranced with the majestic scenery, she wasn't paying any attention to the departing campers.

The former users of the campsite were in such a hurry to leave that they left their ice chest behind.

Jacob laughed. "If those folks came up here to mellow out, it sure didn't work. They have to be the most stressed-out bunch I've ever seen!"

The tires squealed as the van pulled out. Now the Marins could see that two sleeping bags had been left behind along with the ice chest.

"Hey!" Dad yelled at the driver, "you left your sleeping bags and—"

With a grim look on his face, the man looked out the side window of the van. "Never mind them. We're getting out of here while the getting's good."

Mom was becoming a little alarmed at the mysterious haste of the van's departure. "Why, what's the matter?" she called out to the van driver. "Is there something wrong here?"

"Wrong? Yeah, you might say that, lady. There's something *plenty* wrong out there in the woods," the man growled, as he hit the accelerator and sent gravel flying in all directions. Then the van screamed onto the exit road and laid down more rubber as it vanished into the trees.

"Now that's strange, isn't it?" Mom said, as Dad backed the Marins' camper into the empty campsite. "They were lucky enough to spend time in these beautiful mountains—and now they act like the devil himself is after them!"

"Well," Jacob said, "I'm just glad *we* were the ones who got this place! Who cares what happened? Maybe a skunk came out of the woods and scared them or something. Some city folk aren't used to wild things. I'm sure willing to take my chances! Whoa, do you see that lake? It looks like it's covered with diamonds, the way it's sparkling. I bet it's full of fish."

"Yeah," Lettie agreed. When Jacob and Lettie were small, the family had come to Owl Lake three summers in a row. They had had more fun here than anywhere else.

Jacob yanked the fishing gear from the camper and said, "Get ready, everybody! Tonight we're eating some big silver trout, fried over an open flame until it's all crispy and golden."

"Look at the thick woods," Dad said. "I bet there's still a lot of wildlife around. I'm anxious to see deer."

"Yeah," Lettie said, "and bears. Right now a big black bear is probably licking his chops and peeking at us through the trees."

"Well, we'd better keep all the food out of sight, or we might have trouble with the bears," Mom said seriously. "I've heard they come right into camp and help themselves to any food that's around."

"That could be what scared those last folks away," Dad said. "Maybe that's why they were muttering something about there being something wrong in the woods. Could be that a bear chased them!"

"Well, *something* sure scared them," Mom agreed. "Look at these sleeping bags they left behind. They're almost brand new. And this nice ice chest—"

"Did you see what they left over here on the picnic table? It's a real nice knife," Jacob said. "It will be perfect for cleaning the fish. But look—there's *blood* on it!"

# Chapter 2

"*Ewwww!*" Lettie groaned as she looked down at the bloody knife. "Keep that thing away from me. It gives me the creeps."

"They probably used it to cut some meat," Dad said, "or maybe the man accidentally cut himself. I cut myself one time and bled like a stuck pig."

"What do we do with it, Dad?" Lettie asked. "Should we throw it away?"

"Here," Dad said, picking up the knife with a paper towel and dropping it into a plastic bag. "If those folks come back for their stuff, we'll have it ready for them. Otherwise, we'll leave it at the ranger station."

"Why did you pick it up like that, Dad?" Lettie asked.

Dad shrugged. "I don't like to touch strange blood."

"*Ewww,*" Lettie said again, wrinkling her nose. "*Strange blood!* That sounds weird. Hey, Dad, you don't think there's some spooky creature out there in the woods that attacked those people, do you? Like maybe one of those half-ape things you read about?" Lettie was laughing before she finished talking.

"Yeah, right!" Jacob snorted. "I'm *sure* one of those exotic monsters lives right beside Owl Lake. I only hope he didn't eat all the trout."

"Don't they call those big ape-like creatures *Yeti* or something like that?" Lettie asked.

"Nah," Jacob said, "that's the gigantic guy who's supposed to live up in the Himalayas. In other places they call him Meti or Dhookpa or Kang-Mi. The one that's supposed to hang out here in the Sierras is called Bigfoot."

"Okay, you guys," Dad laughed, "enough of that. All those monster stories come from folks who have a little too much to drink and then see a big stranger with a beard. Suddenly it's a monster."

After they helped set up camp, Jacob and Lettie walked to Owl Lake with their fishing gear.

"You think it's all imagination like Dad says?" Lettie asked as they walked down the narrow path.

Jacob shrugged. "Who knows? Grandpa said he saw a mysterious big creature when he used to camp around Eureka, California. He said it sure *looked* real. It was real tall and hairy. . . ."

When they reached the lake, Jacob started fishing for trout while Lettie aimed her camera at the woods. She thought she might get a picture of a deer or something. At the very least she'd get a gorgeous view of the lake and the mountains.

An hour or so later, Jacob had caught several fish, so they headed back to the campsite. Lettie looked at the last picture she had taken with her instant camera. "When we get home I can show my friends what a great place we stayed at," she said. Back at camp, she showed the picture to her mother. "Look at how blue the lake is, Mom. Isn't this a great picture?"

"Oh, that's lovely," Mom said, but then she looked puzzled. "What's that big dark thing in the woods?"

"What dark thing?" Lettie asked, taking her picture back for a closer look. "Wow ... there *is* something. It looks like ... maybe a big bear standing on his hind legs ... or a gorilla ... or maybe it's just a shadow, some kind of optical illusion."

"Let's see that," Dad said, taking a look for himself. "That *does* look something like that Bigfoot thing—not that I believe in any of that nonsense.

Well, it beats me. Maybe somebody threw a hide over a tree branch as a joke. Some people have weird senses of humor, you know."

A short time later, a pickup truck stopped on the little road by the Marins' campsite. A young man leaned out the window and asked, "You folks just settle in here?"

"Sure did!" Dad said. "We felt very lucky to get it. This site is sort of out of the way, so we have privacy. No rowdies nearby blasting their radios and such. I'll be going down to the ranger station in the morning to register. I understand you're only allowed to stay one week in those choice campsites."

"That's right," the young man said. "Did you meet the folks who were here before you? They were odd ducks. They had just used one day of their week . . . then they took off out of here like bats out of hell.

"Oh, excuse me, I'm Kyle Ward. My folks own the cabins down the road. We've got a little restaurant, too. If you guys get tired of camp cooking, come on down and sample some of Mom's chicken and dumplings."

"Thanks," Dad said, "we'll probably get over there before long. We plan to do a lot of hiking. I'm sure we'll get good and hungry for some chicken and dumplings."

"Great!" Kyle said. "And just one more thing—I didn't have much of a chance to talk to those folks who were here before you. But they were really freaking out last night. I don't know *what* was going down!"

The young man smiled then, as if he were embarrassed to go on with the strange story. "But they said some kind of *monster* came after them in the woods. They said that a big furry beast charged one of their sons—and they had to drive it off with a knife!"

Kyle smiled and shook his head before going on. "Of course, some folks watch too many horror movies. Then, when they hear a little noise or see a shadow, they just let their imaginations run away with them. . . ."

# Chapter 3

"Did they call the rangers or the sheriff?" Dad asked. "If anything like that happened to us, the first thing *I'd* do is call the sheriff."

"Yeah," Kyle said, "they called the sheriff all right. He came up here, too. But those folks weren't very believable. They were just talking too crazy. What's a sheriff gonna do with a story about a half-man, half-ape critter coming out of the woods? Anyway, the two guys who had this site before the folks who got spooked—*they* didn't have a bit of trouble!"

Lettie liked Kyle Ward. He seemed nice and friendly and he was very handsome, too. Before school had ended back home, Lettie had broken up with her boyfriend. They didn't have a big fight or anything like that. Somehow they had just grown apart, and now Lettie was feeling a little lonely. She thought it might be fun to get a crush on Kyle. A little romance would surely make this vacation more exciting.

Then Kyle Ward smiled and waved as he drove off.

"Well, these prize-winning fish are all ready to fry," Jacob boasted. "What do you think, Dad? Just have a look at these beauties! Am I a fisherman or what?"

Soon the family sat down to a delicious dinner of fried fish, chips, and a big salad that Mom had brought from home. Lettie thought it was almost funny to think about anything sinister happening in this peaceful place. She couldn't imagine a more serene, beautiful spot anywhere on earth.

After dinner, everybody sat on camp

chairs and watched the sun go down. A pink glow lingered on the patches of snow high on the mountain crevices. Before long the stars came out, clear and sharp. Without the lights and pollution of the city, the stars seemed close enough to touch.

"Tomorrow I want to take a long hike and look for some birds. I understand there are forty species of birds in the mountains," Mom said.

"I think I'll take a little walk right now," Jacob said. "Some of the critters like the raccoon and the 'possum walk by night. Maybe I can see one up close and personal."

"Be careful, Jake," Lettie said, only half jokingly. "If Yeti is lurking out there, he might reach out one of his mammoth hairy arms and pull you into his cave."

"Ha! I told you Yeti lived in the Himalayas, Lettie," Jacob laughed. "It's *Bigfoot* we gotta watch out for."

"Whoever," Lettie said. She hated to go inside the camper when the sky was still so beautiful and the wind was rustling so softly through the pines. How special it was to sit out here and inhale the sweetness of the forest without the rank smell of the neighbor's sports car revving up.

Then, out of the stillness, Lettie heard a twig snap somewhere behind her. It was just a tiny sound, but it startled her. She must have dozed off. That sound had to be Jacob returning. It was nothing more than that. But all the silly talk about Bigfoot and Yeti had planted a tiny seed of fear in Lettie's mind. Of course she didn't *really* think some half-man, half-ape creature was prowling through these woods, but . . .

"How was your walk, Jake?" Lettie asked without turning around. "Did you see any raccoons or 'possums?"

There was no answer. Lettie heard a rattling sound at the other side of the camper. A chill went down her spine. She remembered what Mom had said about bears boldly marching into campsites, searching for any kind of food. Maybe a bear was rummaging around right now. Mom and Dad were inside the camper, probably asleep already. Suddenly, Lettie wished that she was inside, too!

The entrance to the camper was on the other side, the side the strange sounds were coming from. Lettie didn't know what to do. She sure didn't want to become supper for a hungry bear!

"Is it you, Jake?" she called out again, hopefully.

But again, there was no response, although the rattling sounds seemed to have stopped. Lettie got up and walked slowly, peering cautiously around the side of the camper. She couldn't see anything. The path to the door looked clear, so Lettie grabbed the handle and went in. When she closed the door behind her, she was breathing hard.

Then Lettie heard the funny noises again, but she was safely inside the camper. It must be some pesky little 'possum or a skunk, she thought. *Something* was making those noises!

Could it be Jacob? Was Jacob so silly that he was deliberately sneaking around making noises as a practical joke? That was Jacob when he was 15— but he was 20 now. He was a serious biology student in college with plans to go into research. He didn't do practical jokes anymore. At least Lettie didn't *think* he did. . . .

Suddenly the card table the Marins had set up outside for dinner collapsed with a terrible clatter. Lettie peeked out and shouted, "Mom! Dad! There's something going on out there!"

Mom and Dad ran out of the small bedroom in the rear part of the camper.

"What's up?" Dad asked, looking sleepy and confused.

Lettie was already feeling foolish. Maybe some bits of fish under the card table had attracted small animals. "Something really spooked me. 'Possums are probably out there having a midnight snack or something, Dad," Lettie said.

"Well, let's take a look," Dad said, getting out a flashlight. He reached for the door.

"Don't go out just yet, Dad!" Lettie said suddenly. She had a creepy, scary feeling that something dangerous was waiting outside. She didn't know what, but she was afraid—and it wasn't like her to be afraid.

Dad smiled reassuringly at Lettie. "It's okay, honey," he said. "Remember when we went to the Philippines to visit Grandpa? Remember how scared we were when we heard those long-tailed monkeys screaming from the trees? We were frightened because we didn't know what it was, but it turned out that we weren't in any danger."

Lettie smiled, too. It had been so exciting for her and Jacob to see the land of their ancestors, to eat *lumpia* and *pancit* at her grandparents' house. Probably some innocent little animal was making a ruckus here, too—just like the long-tailed monkeys whose cries had been so alarming.

Dad looked around the area outside the trailer and found nothing. But then Mom peered out the door and asked him, "Where's Jacob? Shouldn't he be back from his walk by now?"

"Yeah," Dad said. "I hope he didn't get lost when he was out there roaming around. That's easy to do in unfamiliar territory. It must be seven years since we've been here at Owl Lake."

"I'm really getting worried," Mom said. "Jacob said he was just taking a short walk. He promised to come right back. What could be keeping him?"

# Chapter 4

"Don't worry," Dad said. "Lettie and I will take a look and do some hollering for him to come home. You know how Jacob is. When he finds something that interests him, he loses all track of time."

"Wait!" Lettie cried, spotting a distant figure coming toward the camper at a very slow pace. "Isn't that Jake? I think he's coming now."

"Oh, thank heaven!" Mom sighed in relief. "I couldn't even *think* of going to bed until he got in."

"Dad," Lettie said in a suddenly tense voice, "something must be wrong. Look how slowly he's walking!"

Lettie and her parents ran across the meadow to meet Jacob. Lettie got to her brother first. "Jake!" Lettie cried. "What happened out there? Your shirt is all torn, and you look like you've been in a fight! Are you okay?"

"Man," Jacob said, "I don't know what hit me! I spotted raccoon tracks coming from a little stream, and I was following them when *wham*—something heavy came down on the back of my head and sent me flying."

"Jacob!" Mom cried, putting her arms around him. "Are you sure you're all right? It looks like something has been clawing at your shirt. And you've got deep scratches on your arms!"

"Were you attacked by someone?" Dad asked in a shocked voice. "Do you think someone was hiding out there and struck you from behind?"

"Dad, I'm not sure what happened. It all came down so fast. I was walking along just fine one minute, and the next minute I got hit. Maybe it was only a tree branch falling . . . but I had the feeling that someone—or *something*— was ripping at me when I was down on the ground. . . ." Jacob said.

There was blood in Jacob's hair and some long scratches on his arm, but otherwise he was all right. Dad got right on the cellular phone to call the sheriff. "If there's a criminal out there attacking people, he's got to be stopped! Remember the last people who camped here? They said they fought with some kind of intruder, too. Maybe there *was* some truth to their crazy-sounding story!"

The sheriff and an ambulance arrived quickly. The paramedics gave Jacob first aid for his minor wounds, but he refused to go to the hospital. "I'm not spending my vacation in the ER," he said firmly. "I'm not dizzy or sick to my stomach or anything like that. Believe me, I feel okay."

"Well," the paramedic said, "if you get a headache or start experiencing dizziness or any bleeding from the nose or mouth, you or your folks should call us immediately."

"I feel *fine!*" Jacob insisted.

The sheriff wrote down Jacob's story with a look of bemused puzzlement on his face. "If you can't say for sure that a person attacked you, I don't see how we can go looking for an assailant," he said. "We can't arrest tree branches. We need solid information."

"I just don't know what happened," Jacob said.

After the sheriff drove away, Lettie remembered what Kyle Ward had told them about the previous campers being attacked by a strange, vicious creature. The sheriff said that he knew about that, but Lettie could tell that he didn't believe it for a minute. He thought hysteria was taking over. He'd seen it before. When one person reports a weird happening, pretty soon *everybody* claims to have seen the same weird thing.

"I'm not stupid enough to think the Abominable Snowman bopped me on the head," Jacob said. "The last thing I remember, I was crouching down looking at the animal tracks. Then I probably straightened up and hit my head on a tree branch. That makes the most sense."

"But why was your shirt ripped up so badly?" Mom asked.

"I don't know, Mom! Maybe some of the branches were sharp or thorny," Jacob said in exasperation.

Dad beamed his flashlight around the campsite again and finally said, "Well, I think it's best that we all go to bed now. We *have* had raccoons or 'possums messing around here, I expect. And as for what got you, Jacob, I'm not discounting a bear. Maybe you shouldn't have gone off by yourself in the dark like that."

Lettie walked into the camper with her brother. "Bears don't hit people over the head." she said softly. *"People do that. Or—"*

Jacob gave his sister a wry look and said, "Or half-man, half-animal guys like Bigfoot, eh?"

After breakfast the next morning, the Marins went hiking. They walked the trail Jacob had taken the night before, looking all around for clues about the incident. Before long, Jacob found the exact place where he had fallen. A button from his shirt lay in the dirt. "Look here! This is where my button got ripped off," he said.

"I don't see any low branches," Lettie said, looking up into the trees.

"Come over here," Mom said. She was kneeling on the ground, looking down intently. Since there was a mountain stream nearby, the earth around the area was soft enough to show footprints quite clearly. "Are these tracks of some kind?"

Jacob knelt beside Mom. "Yeah,

these prints look like somebody was walking barefoot," he said.

"They're awfully *big*," Dad said.

A shudder went down Lettie's spine. Of course, the first thing she thought of was Bigfoot!

"This footprint is over twelve inches long," Jacob said, "and look, there's another one. It must have gone back into the woods. See? The footprints vanish in the pine needle carpet right over here."

"*It?*" Dad repeated. "What are you saying, Jacob? Do you really believe it was a *creature* that attacked you?"

"No, Dad," Jacob said quickly, "but it *is* weird. A couple of years ago I was reading about these mountain creatures that people are always talking about. Way back in 1957, villagers in Nepal said that five people were battered to death by Yetis in the mountains."

"My goodness!" Mom cried. "I always thought those things didn't exist. Now you're telling me they've actually killed people?"

"Maybe it was something else that really happened," Jacob said, "but this article I read also told about a Norwegian guy. He was hiking in Sikkim in the Himalayas when a Yeti attacked him and almost busted his shoulder. The man swore to it."

"Well, I know one thing," Dad said. "Nobody in this family is going out alone anymore. There's safety in numbers. We're not going to give up our beautiful campsite and go hightailing it out of here like those other folks did. But let's not be foolhardy, either."

# Chapter 5

That night the Marins hiked down to the little restaurant operated by Kyle Ward's parents. There were a dozen small redwood cabins clustered nearby. The restaurant was located in a large old house that had been converted.

"Four orders of delicious chicken and dumplings coming up," Kyle said. "Not to mention corn and string beans and Mom's famous biscuits made from scratch with sweet butter!"

"You got it!" Dad laughed.

Kyle came over to their table while they waited for their order. Jacob told him what had happened last night.

"That's really strange," Kyle said. "Musta been darn scary, too."

"How long have you and your

family lived around here?" Lettie asked the handsome young man.

"Oh, we've been here ever since I was just a little kid. I've been home schooled. I'm eighteen now, and I've never seen the inside of a real school! When I go off to college this fall, it's going to be quite an experience for me," Kyle said.

"Have you . . . uh . . . ever seen strange creatures around here?" Lettie asked. "Like . . . you know, that thing they call Bigfoot?"

"No, I've never seen anything like that—but I've heard stories. From time to time, campers talk about seeing stuff. Like the folks who couldn't wait to get away from your campsite— something sure scared *them* half to death," Kyle said.

"But how about the guys who had the campsite before them?" Dad recalled. "You said they didn't have any problems."

"Right. They were two young guys in a beat-up old van. They spent their week in a dome tent. Never left the camp at all. They weren't real friendly. They never came here to eat. I figured they were short of money. Their van was in bad shape and their tent was all ragged, but they were good campers. Always cleaning up, raking the campsite to keep it neat," Kyle said.

"Well, I think I got beaned by a tree branch, and all this Bigfoot stuff is just so much nonsense," Jacob said. "I'm feeling great now, and eating a big plate of homestyle chicken is going to make me feel even better!"

The next afternoon, the Marins went out hiking again. As they arrived back at camp, Lettie gasped, "Look! Somebody has been digging big holes around our camper!"

"How about that?" Jacob said. "Looks like they tried to fill up the holes again, too."

"Now what's this all about?" Mom asked, frowning.

Dad walked around, studying the fresh piles of loose dirt. "Seems like somebody must have been looking for something," he said.

"You think gold is buried around here . . . or some other kind of treasure?" Lettie asked excitedly.

"That must be it," Jacob chimed in sarcastically, "and maybe some pirate ghosts are harassing the campers who come here so they can dig in peace."

The Marins were so intent on the holes that they didn't even notice when a man with curly gray hair came walking up. He didn't look more than about 40, and his beard was more red than gray. His sun-browned face was unlined and he wore a bandanna around his head. He carried a stout walking stick, and smiled cheerfully as he greeted the Marin family. "Howdy there, folks!" he called out.

"Hello," Dad said. "We just came back from a hike, and this is what we found. It looks like a dozen giant gophers have been digging around here. But we're pretty sure gophers didn't do it."

The man nodded. "Nope. Gophers don't make a mess like that. Oh, let me introduce myself. Name's Siskin. I travel through the mountains all year long, camping here and there. Now, digging like you see there—why, there's just one explanation for that," he said confidently.

After Dad introduced his family, he asked, "So what *is* the explanation, if you don't mind my asking?"

The man smiled and said, "UFOs."

"UFOs?" Jacob repeated in disbelief. He was trying hard not to laugh at this preposterous stranger, although he was certainly tempted to.

"Sure," Siskin said matter-of-factly. "They been landing up here in the mountains right along. They're taking soil samples. No doubt about it. That's what you're seeing there."

"What do they look like?" Lettie asked, fighting her own amusement.

"The UFOs?" Siskin said. "Oh, you know that. Lots of folks have seen them by now. The government tries to cover it all up, but there's thousands of us seen them for ourselves. The UFOs are shaped like discs, or platters, or whatever. Everybody knows that by now.

"The *fellas* on the ships, though . . . Only I and a very few others have seen them, talked to them. All of them are covered with hair, whitish gray like a husky dog. They have thin lips and dark eyes. Nothing extraordinary."

Lettie glanced at her father. They were both thinking the same thing. Siskin was a pretty strange fellow—but there could very well be a method in his madness. He looked like a man who loved the wilderness and wanted to see the natural landscape left alone. No doubt he resented all the visitors intruding on the lives of the local animals. Surely he had made up his wild story in the hope of scaring away all the campers he met.

Maybe it was Siskin who had crept up behind Jacob and knocked him down, Siskin who disturbed the campsite by knocking over the card table—and who knows? Maybe it was Siskin himself who dug the holes.

# Chapter 6

"So tell me, Mr. Siskin," Dad asked calmly, "do you think there could be something . . . *special* about this campsite? Some special reason the . . . uh . . . UFO guys might not want people camping here?"

"Yeah, sure," Siskin said readily, adding to the Marins' suspicion that the man would just as soon they leave. "Some places have special vibrations. Lot of places in New Mexico are like that. Connections to the alien folk. It'd be a whole lot better if nobody ever camped right here."

"So you think we should move on?" Jacob asked.

"Well now, that's up to you," Siskin said with a serious look on his face.

"You can take your chances if you like. Who's gonna stop you? But those aliens can get pretty aggressive. I've seen them work. They never bother *me*, of course. That's 'cause I agree with them that the wilderness ought to be left alone. But you folks just suit yourselves." With that, Siskin nodded farewell and strolled off.

"What a bigtime scammer!" Dad laughed when the man was out of earshot. "He's one of those guys who'd do just about anything to keep the wilderness pristine. He'd say *anything* to chase people off!"

Jacob nodded. "Yeah, but . . . I halfway agree with him, I guess. It bothers me to see so much trash thrown around. Like people tossing beer cans in the big meadow where the deer graze," he said.

"*We* don't do that," Lettie said defensively. "We put every bit of our trash in the barrels."

"Yeah, but lots of people aren't so careful—as you know. When dozens and then hundreds of campers show up, the wilderness gets pretty much trashed," Jacob said.

"But, honey," Mom said, "what good is such a lovely place if nobody ever comes to see it?"

"Yeah," Jacob said, "I know you're right, Mom."

"Well, anyway," Dad said, "now that we've got a pretty good idea who our pest is, we'd better be vigilant. If Siskin comes around again and causes any trouble, we need to call the sheriff right away."

In the early evening, Dad got busy barbecuing steaks. Soon the delicious aroma of roasting meat blotted out the heavy pine smell. Everybody sat on camp chairs with their plates on their knees, and Dad grinned broadly. "How about it, guys? Is this the good life or what?" he asked.

The Marins went to bed early that night. About midnight, however, the silence was shattered by a series of loud, unearthly shrieks. "What on earth!" Mom cried, sitting up in bed.

"Looks like old Siskin is on the job again," Dad grumbled. "I suppose he's rigged up a loudspeaker out there. Now he must be playing Halloween tapes! The crazy old coot. Well, I've had about enough of this!"

Lettie peered out the window of the camper. All she saw was darkness, but the blood-curdling shrieking continued. Lettie snuggled into her robe and thought about her comfortable bedroom at home. She finally understood why those other campers had taken off! Having a beautiful remote camping site with a view of Owl Lake was great— but not if a nightly horror show was the price they had to pay!

"Mom, Dad, let's just get out of here," Lettie groaned. "I'm sick of whatever the heck is going on here!"

"I'll be darned if I'm going to turn tail and run!" Dad exclaimed. "We can't allow a little weirdo like Siskin to drive us away and ruin our vacation."

Dad and Jacob went outside with their flashlights, shining the beams toward the woods where the shrieks seemed to be coming from. "Hey, Siskin," Dad shouted. "*Knock it off!* You aren't scaring anybody. You're just making a fool of yourself!"

When the shrieks stopped, Dad grinned triumphantly. "See? We've called his bluff. I'm not faulting the guy for caring about the wilderness, but this play-acting is going too far," Dad said.

Lettie breathed a sigh of relief. She had actually begun to believe there was some furry creature lying in wait to tear them apart! Now that Dad's stern voice had ended the shrieks, she suddenly had no more doubt that they had been the work of a trickster.

Dad was still grinning when he came back inside the camper. "I've been standing up to bullies all my life," he said proudly. "Way back in grade school a few wise guys liked to pick on some of us. But the minute we stood up to them, they deflated like a balloon pricked with a pin!"

Lettie decided that the Yeti or Bigfoot or whoever was out there was nothing more than a *wannabe*. Of course, it was safe to go outside and spend some time looking up at the beautiful night sky, finding her favorite constellations! Since the phony shrieks had already woken her up, she thought she might as well go outside for some stargazing right now.

"Come on in, Lettie," Mom called when she saw her daughter step out the door. "We need to get back to sleep. Tomorrow we're going to hike around Eagle Mountain, and we're planning to get an early start."

Lettie turned to go back into the camper—but then someone grabbed her and clamped a hand over her mouth! Lettie tried to scream, but she couldn't get out a sound. Before she knew it, she was rapidly being dragged away! She couldn't fight her attacker off. He was too strong.

Lettie heard her mother's annoyed voice, "*Come on in, Lettie!* We've had enough excitement for one night."

For a split second, Lettie glimpsed the arm around her waist as it pulled her toward the thick woods. Her heart almost stopped. The arm was huge, hairy, and definitely not human!

"Oh, no!" Lettie thought to herself. "It can't be true!" The mysterious hulking creature found in mountains all over the world was actually *here* at Owl Lake! The beast who had battered the men to death in Nepal now had *her*! And it was dragging her deeper and deeper into the woods!

# Chapter 7

Lettie realized that she had to do something fast. With all her might she kicked back with her right leg. She was a good soccer player, and she knew she had a powerful kick. But the thing didn't even seem to notice. Then Lettie opened her mouth and tried to bite the hand clamped around her face. When she bit down on what seemed to be a finger, the thing holding her let out a grunt of pain.

But, relentlessly, the thing continued to drag Lettie farther into the woods. She couldn't believe this was happening to her! Only a few days ago she had been graduating from high school and looking forward to a wonderful summer. First, the camping trip in the high Sierras, and then a trip back to the Philippines to visit her cousins and grandparents again. Her life was just *beginning*—and now it was all coming to an end!

How could such a hideous creature have lived in these lovely mountains for so long without anybody knowing it? How could the park rangers have missed it?

Lettie aimed another sharp kick and heard a grunt of pain. For a split second the grip on Lettie's mouth loosened up. "Help!" Lettie screamed shrilly. *"Help!"*

Now Lettie could see Dad and Jacob coming toward them. The moment she'd screamed, they'd started running.

The creature was apparently fearful of being caught. It freed Lettie and turned to scamper away. Lettie turned and got a good look at it. It was over six feet tall, as foul smelling as a mildewed old towel at a gym, and had dark, matted hair. Running at a furious speed back into the woods, it disappeared just as Dad and Jacob reached her.

"Sweetheart, are you okay?" Dad asked, taking Lettie in his arms and holding her tight.

"I'm okay, Dad, but it was *awful*! Did you get a good look at that thing? It was so horrible. It just came out of nowhere and grabbed me. I couldn't believe it. How could nobody know about a horrible monster attacking people in the woods?" Lettie cried.

"Man, I can hardly believe it, either," Jacob said. "Sure, we've *talked* about stuff like this, but I thought it was all a myth or a joke. Now I bet that creature was what hit me, too."

Then Mom came running toward them, panting and white-faced. "Is she okay? Is she okay? Oh, Lettie, baby—"

"I'm *fine*, Mom," Lettie assured her. "The thing held me real tight, but I kicked back at it and made it let me go. I'm not really hurt or anything. I just want to take a nice hot shower and get the smell of that nasty hairy thing off my pajamas and my body."

"Good for you that you were able to kick it so hard," Jacob said.

"Yeah," Lettie said. "I guess I've got a pretty good kick!"

"Well, we're not staying here any longer," Dad said. "I know when I'm licked. After you get cleaned up, Lettie, we're pulling out. I've had enough of this. I'm not risking my family another minute! I'm calling the sheriff, and he better get on this fast!"

Soon after dawn, the sheriff arrived at the campsite. After taking Lettie's statement, he and his deputy walked all around the place looking for footprints and other evidence. When the sheriff returned, he said, "I've lived in this place for 47 years. I grew up right here in the foothills of these mountains. I've been sheriff here for 11 years. In all that time, I've never seen any solid evidence of a Bigfoot kind of creature bothering people. You always hear wild tales— mostly after a camper's had too much to drink. But nothing has ever convinced me that such critters exist."

"Well, I saw it and it grabbed me," Lettie insisted, "and I've never been so scared in all my life."

Then Jacob gave the sheriff the snapshot Lettie had taken when they first arrived at Owl Lake. He studied the figure that looked like a furry creature standing in the forest. But still the sheriff looked skeptical. "Well, I don't know. But it's clear," he said, "that *somebody* assaulted this young lady last night—and I assure you that we intend to get to the bottom of it!"

"Sheriff," Jacob said, "there's a guy came around here yesterday, a fella who called himself Siskin. Maybe you know him—a guy with curly gray hair and a red-gray beard? He seemed to resent people camping around these mountains. He told us some wild story about UFOs landing up here with big hairy aliens aboard. I think he was trying to scare us off. I wonder if you know anybody like that. Maybe he's a local character?"

The sheriff shook his head. "I never saw anybody like that around here. I know everybody in the mountains, too. Can't recall ever seeing such a fella."

"He said he's a drifter who camps all over the mountains," Lettie said.

When the sheriff left, the Marins packed up all their gear and pulled out of the campsite. They drove down the road to Kyle Ward's place, rented one of their camper spaces, and hooked up electricity and water.

"It's sure nice having you folks," Kyle said, "but I'm real sorry you got chased from your pretty campsite, though. That must have been a pretty horrible experience, Lettie."

The Marins went into the restaurant and had their breakfast. Lettie sat at a little table with Kyle and had coffee and a cheese Danish. The more she saw of Kyle, the nicer and more attractive she found him to be.

"Do you think it's possible that the thing that grabbed me was one of those Bigfoot monsters, Kyle?" Lettie asked. "It was so huge and smelly! And it seemed inhumanly strong as it was dragging me into the woods."

Kyle smiled sheepishly, as if he didn't want to hurt Lettie's feelings by doubting her story. But it was clear that he really couldn't accept the Bigfoot story. "I believe somebody grabbed you all right, Lettie—but it must have been a guy in a gorilla suit or something like that. But no, I don't really think there's a half-man, half-ape lurking in our mountains."

"But what's going on, Kyle? The last people who camped there were scared away, too. Now *we're* being driven away. Do you think somebody just wants the site to himself? Or just hates campers being there?" Lettie asked.

"Well," Kyle replied, "a lot of people who live around here are getting tired of so many outsiders in the mountains. Every year more and more people come. There are some local folk who freak on the subject. Newspaper stories call them *tree-huggers*. But they're really just folks who are upset about the wilderness being destroyed.

"Every summer more and more trash is being dumped in the streams and rivers, and more animals get their feet caught in poptop soda cans." Kyle continued. "It's like people who visit here just don't care. A few of the local people just go nuts, I guess. At night all you hear are radios and CD players blasting away. Every year there are fewer birds, fewer animals—"

"It sounds like *you're* one of the

people who doesn't like all the camping here, Kyle," Lettie said, hearing the unmistakable passion in the young man's voice.

"I love the mountains. I'd like them to stay the same, sure. But I know that's impossible. I love people, too. I want them to come out and enjoy themselves—if only folks would be more considerate," Kyle said. Then he brightened. "I've got an idea. What do you say about the two of us taking a hike today? We'll take the Osprey Trail to the lookout point. Then we can use my binoculars to see if there's any action at your old camp."

"Yeah," Lettie said, jumping at the idea. "A strange guy came by yesterday trying to scare us off by talking about UFOs. He called himself Siskin. Maybe we'll see him sitting at our empty campsite, celebrating that we're gone."

"Siskin?" Kyle repeated. "That's the name of a bird, you know. *Pine siskin*.

Used to be big flocks of maybe a hundred birds in a tree. But for the past couple of years, there haven't been nearly that many."

When Lettie told her parents of her plan to hike Osprey Trail with Kyle, Dad frowned and shook his head. "I don't want you putting yourself at anymore risk, Lettie. We've had enough frights on this vacation. First Jacob getting knocked down, then you being dragged off—"

"Oh, you don't have anything to worry about," Kyle reassured him. "We won't be taking any chances, sir. We'll just hike up Osprey Trail, take a look, and come back down. For sure, we won't be confronting anybody."

"All right, I guess," Dad said.

"Please don't worry, Mr. Marin," Kyle said again. "Believe me, I'll take good care of Lettie!"

Lettie glowed at the tone of his voice. It sounded like maybe Kyle liked her as much as she liked him!

# Chapter 8

Backpacks on and hiking sticks in hand, Lettie and Kyle started up Osprey Trail. All along the path there were markers telling about the wildlife in the area and offering other interesting historical tidbits.

"Look, Kyle. Here's a marker that says this path was part of the Emigrant Trail to California in the 1840s and 1860s," Lettie said.

"Yeah, I've heard that some of the forty-niners came this way," Kyle said. "It was pretty dangerous in those days. Some of them froze to death in the high country blizzards."

"Maybe some of the forty-niners buried their gold down at the campsite where we were," Lettie suggested.

"I don't think so," Kyle laughed. "If miners were lucky enough to find gold, they didn't bury it on the way home!"

It was a beautiful trail. Lettie was thrilled to see some hawks flying from the high cliffs. She also saw last winter's snow still sparkling from crevices rarely touched by the sun.

"Here's the lookout point," Kyle said at last. "Look down that way. We can see your old campsite from here."

Lettie took the second pair of binoculars Kyle had brought, and they both looked down at the camp.

"Nobody down there now," Kyle said. "Boy, you sure left that camp in good condition. It looks like nobody has been there in ages."

"We always leave campsites like that. Dad always says that the next people who arrive are entitled to as clean a place as we found," Lettie said.

Kyle showed Lettie a map of the whole area that pointed out where all the scenic spots were. The campsites were clearly visible. Lettie could see that the one they had was unusual in its privacy and clear view of Owl Lake. "Maybe some guys harassed us just so they could get our spot for themselves," Lettie laughed, although she was only half joking.

"I don't think so. It had to be a more serious reason than that. Grabbing you like that is a serious assault, Lettie," Kyle said. "It burns me up that anyone would do such a thing to a nice person like you."

"You've been so kind to us, Kyle. Do you get to know all the campers around here really well?" Lettie asked.

"No," Kyle said with a little smile, "just the ones with pretty daughters."

Then he laughed. "Actually, I *do* try to make friends with the campers. I want them all to come down to eat at Mom's restaurant."

Lettie peered through the binoculars

again, not expecting to see anything. But now two men were moving onto the campsite. "Look, Kyle, those guys are taking our camp!" she said.

"Hey," Kyle said, looking into his binoculars, "those are the same guys who had it before the people who got scared off. See the ratty van I told you about? And look, they're unloading their dome tent."

Lettie stared through the binoculars at the two young men busily setting up camp. With their very short military-style hair and hard faces, they looked like the kind of men you wouldn't want to get into an argument with.

Kyle turned the binoculars in a wide arc. "I don't see Bigfoot anywhere. Just those guys."

"I bet those two are glad we left so quickly, huh?" Lettie said. "I wonder how they knew we would. When Dad signed up at the camp, we were given seven full days. Those guys must have been hanging around somewhere, ready to grab the campsite if we moved out. Hey, Kyle, you don't think—"

Kyle looked again through the binoculars. "Oh-oh. They got binoculars, too, Lettie, and they're looking up this way. I guess the sun on our binoculars must have glinted and caught their eye. They saw us looking down on them. Now they don't look too happy that someone's spying on them."

"I guess maybe we'd better head back," Lettie said, suddenly feeling nervous and cold.

"Wait! You know, I just remembered something," Kyle said. "My grandfather told me a story about something that happened up in these mountains years and years ago . . . around 1970, I think. An armored car robber was hiding around here then. Supposedly he had stashed a million bucks in a real pretty spot. People said the money was in four boxes. He figured to come back for the money when he got out of jail. Over time the story became kind of a legend. But the guy died in jail. I wonder if those jokers down there got hold of one of the maps the robber was supposed to have drawn. What if the money is buried at that campsite!"

"That would certainly be a good reason to want the campsite all to themselves," Lettie said nervously. "Come on, Kyle. Let's go back down the trail. Those guys keep looking and pointing up this way."

"Yeah, right," Kyle agreed, but then he took one more look through his binoculars. "Wait! They've stopped unloading their gear, Lettie. One of them is still looking up here at us. The other guy, he's digging in his knapsack for . . . *a gun*! If they know anything about the trails around here, they'll probably try to head us off. Oh, lord, Lettie! We could be in big trouble!"

 # Chapter 9

"Can't we get back to your cabin another way?" Lettie asked. There was nothing but fear in her voice now.

"No, Osprey Trail ends up against a granite mountain. If those guys are heading to the head of the trail right now, they're gonna meet us before we're halfway down," Kyle said.

Lettie turned numb. The men had taken a big risk by attacking her and Jacob. If they were willing to wear smelly gorilla suits to frighten people off the campsite, they really meant business. If they thought they were on the verge of finding a million dollars in loot, they were probably willing to do *anything* to keep their plans on target!

"What are we going to do, Kyle?"

Lettie asked in a small, scared voice.

"I sure don't want to run smack into those guys. They look more dangerous than Bigfoot ever dreamed of being. I'm afraid we'll have to climb up on some pretty treacherous rocks and then try to cut across the mountain. There's no trail where we're going—but it's the only way to avoid them," Kyle said.

"Okay, just lead the way," Lettie said anxiously.

Within a minute, they had left the wide, pleasant Osprey Trail with its camper-friendly markers and lookout points and started climbing over boulders. Instead of going south toward the cabins, though, they were heading east. Eventually they would cut south again—but only after they had lost their pursuers.

"If we play our cards right, we'll come down right behind our cabins and they'll never see us," Kyle said, "but the terrain is really rough. Are you going to be okay with all of this, Lettie?"

"Sure," Lettie said confidently, "I hike all the time." That was not entirely true. Sure, she often took nice long nature walks along wide, well-kept trails back home. But never in her life had she scrambled over such enormous boulders as these!

Still, Lettie gamely followed Kyle as they clawed their way over the huge granite boulders, sometimes inching along on their stomachs. Lettie nicked her knee a couple of times and blood leaked through her jeans. She didn't say anything about it, however, and she hoped Kyle didn't notice.

When they reached a ravine, Kyle gasped, "Oh, man, I never counted on there being so much water!"

"You mean we've got to get across that ravine?" Lettie groaned as she gaped at the raging torrent at the bottom of the gorge. "The water is so *deep*! And look how fast it's moving!"

It looked like the flooded control channels Lettie had seen on TV—the kind that swept people away if they were foolish enough to come too close.

"I don't know any other way to get across," Kyle said. "I'd forgotten about the heavy rains we had last week. They *really* flooded the rivers. Hey, maybe we could use rope harnesses and *swing* across, Lettie."

"Are you crazy?" Lettie cried. "I'm not that Tarzan guy who grabs vines and flies over the jungle. I don't want to fall and drown! Look, the river is full of tree branches and stuff. And the water is moving much too fast!"

"But Lettie, we've *got* to get across somehow. Those creeps are on their way up Osprey Trail right now. They could very well come this way, looking for us. If they confront us here, they'll probably decide it's a good idea just to shove us into the river!" Kyle said.

"But I can't swing on a rope across

the river," Lettie insisted. "I just *can't!*"

"Look, I'll make a real strong harness. I've got a good rope in my backpack. I always carry it when I go hiking. We'll tie one end of the rope to that tree there and I'll give you a good push—just like you push a little kid on a swing. You'll make it to the other side easy. Look, it's not that far across. It's only about six or seven feet."

"Kyle, I swear to you—I'll fall right into the gorge and drown!" Lettie almost cried.

Suddenly Kyle's face took on an ugly, insulting expression. "So, you're *chicken!*" he taunted. "Well, I'm not surprised. Most girls are. That's why girls can't do as much stuff as guys can. You're just chicken."

"I am *not* chicken!" Lettie shouted, as rage quickly replaced her fear. "Okay, tie the stupid harness on me— but if I drown it will be all your fault, Kyle Ward!"

Kyle tied the harness around Lettie's shoulders. Then she walked back from the edge and, following his instructions, got a good running start. Kyle's idea was that the momentum of the leap would carry her across the narrow crevice to the other side.

"Remember," Kyle shouted, "even if you fall, the rope will catch you before you hit the river. I promise that I'll pull you up to safety, Lettie. Now *go, girl*! You can do it!"

Lettie's legs felt shaky and weak. She scarcely breathed as she soared over the crevice and landed in the meadow on the opposite side. When she hit the ground, she rolled in the grass, winded. Then she quickly unhitched the harness and threw it back to Kyle. In a moment, he did the same thing, landing safely beside her.

"Let's go now!" Kyle said.

Lettie was trembling. She couldn't believe what she had just done. But she also had a great sense of elation. She had met a terrible challenge and gotten through it. Now the ravine separated them from two dangerous men who were making their way up the trail.

After scrambling over more boulders and brush for another half-hour, Lettie and Kyle finally came down behind the Wards' cabins.

Lettie's father called the sheriff and reported that two armed men were on Osprey Trail. He told the sheriff that he suspected that these were the two men who had been behind the harassment campaign all along.

An hour or so later, the sheriff and his deputy caught the two men and checked them out. Sure enough, they turned out to be parole violators with long records. They had a map on them that showed the location of the million-dollar loot. It was buried at a campsite very much like the one they had just re-occupied. And in one of the men's backpacks, the sheriff found a filthy gorilla suit and a CD player with a Halloween shriek album.

"Likely there's no loot buried there," the sheriff said later, when he was having dinner with the Marins at Kyle's mom's place. "Those poor fools got themselves in a mess of trouble for nothing. But at least we know now that the mountains are safe. I mean, we know there are no strange monsters running around, anyway."

"We could go back to our beautiful campsite now," Dad said, hopefully.

"I don't know," Mom said, worry in her eyes. "I sort of like it here. Let's just let things be."

"Well, kids, now that the sheriff has cleared out the bad guys, what do you want to do? Let's at least hike down to the campsite and have a look at what we lost," Dad said cheerfully.

"Okay, why not?" Jacob replied.

Kyle and Lettie walked together, holding hands. After giving it some thought, Lettie had forgiven Kyle for calling her names. He knew it was the only way to get Lettie to cross the river. As they walked along they saw that the sun was setting and the sky was darkening quickly.

"Look, there's something very bright in the sky," Jacob said.

"Hmmm. Must be the fading sun reflecting off the wing of a plane," Dad said as he looked up.

When they were about 300 yards from the campsite, they saw that strange guy Siskin standing there. He was looking skyward with an expression of deep concentration on his face. He seemed to be *communicating* in some way with something in the sky.

Lettie began to tingle all over.

It wasn't that she *believed* in UFOs, of course. She didn't really.

But she heard herself saying, "Dad,

let's not go any closer—let's go back to the Wards' cabins."

"Why, sweetheart?" Dad asked.

"Oh, it's so beautiful there—it's almost *sacred*. Like all the animals have reclaimed it somehow. . . ." Lettie's voice trailed off.

That sounded good to Dad. It had been a very long day and everyone was tired. They turned and walked back toward the cabins. The amazing sounds and smells of nature were all around them. They never looked back.

# COMPREHENSION QUESTIONS

**RECALL**

1. The Marin family planned the camping trip as a family celebration. What two events were they celebrating?

2. Jacob took a walk the first night they were in camp. What was he hoping to see?

**ANALYZING CHARACTERS**

1. Which two words could describe Jacob? Explain your thinking.
   - *knowledgeable*
   - *timid*
   - *environmentalist*

2. Which two words could describe Kyle? Explain your thinking.
   - *superstitious*
   - *friendly*
   - *resourceful*

**VOCABULARY**

1. What did Mr. Marin mean when he said they should all be careful but not *foolhardy*?

2. What is an *isolated* campsite?

3. Lettie couldn't believe that something *sinister* could happen in such a peaceful setting. What does *sinister* mean?

**DRAWING CONCLUSIONS**

1. What conclusion did Siskin draw about the holes that had been dug around the Marins' campsite?

2. What conclusion did the Marins draw about Siskin?

3. What conclusion did Lettie come to when she was dragged into the woods?